“I need dinner,” the man thinks to himself.

I0820460

He has a pot, a spoon, and a rock.

"I can cook broth with a rock," he yells.

I just need carrots, leeks, garlic, and a pinch of pepper.

The man sips the broth.

“It just needs a bag of lentils,” he adds.

The man spoons
the broth into cups.

Yum! Rock broth is the best!